THE

S

THE TURKEY THAT VOTED FOR CHRISTMAS

MADELEINE COOK
&
SAMARA HARDY

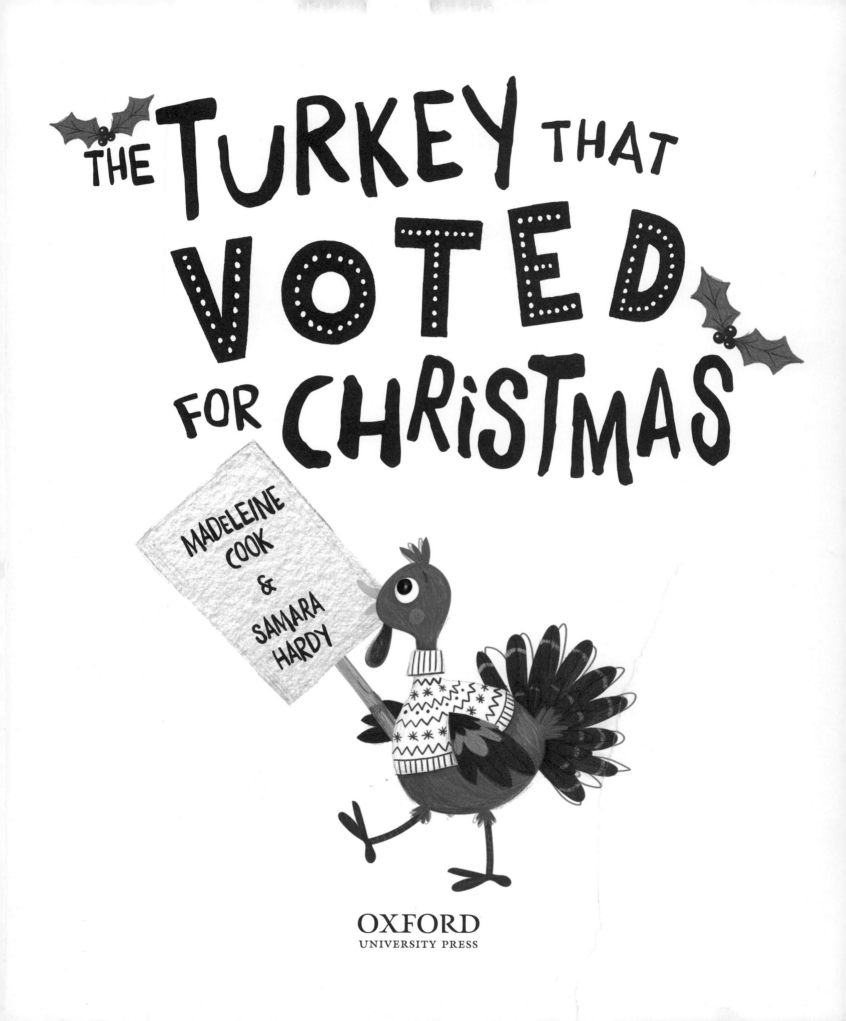

OXFORD
UNIVERSITY PRESS

The animals of Pear Tree Farm loved to vote.

They voted for who baked the best cakes.

They voted for who was the best dancer.

But when it came to Christmas, all the turkeys voted . . .

'NO!' Well, all the turkeys except Timmy Turkey, that is. 'Why do turkeys never vote for Christmas?' he asked.

NO

NO

NO

NO

Grandad

Grandma

Dad

Mum

'Farmer Carver might have something to do with why they vote NO!'

NO

NO

NO

Nana

NO

YES

Gramps

NO

Uncle Bernard

Timmy

Uncle Matthew

'Because I say so,' said Mum.
'Your mum knows best,' added Uncle Bernard and Uncle Matthew. Dad, Grandad, Grandma, Gramps, and Nana all agreed.

But Timmy **REALLY** wished there could be Christmas on Pear Tree Farm.

Dasher

Noel

Carol

Gabriel

Holly

PEAR TREE FARM

So he decided to hold a proper Christmas election. First of all, he needed to know who he could count on for support.
So he called a meeting.

'Put your hand up if you LOVE Christmas,' said Timmy.

'I love Christmas too!'

Noel counted five hands.

Then Carol pointed out that Noel hadn't counted his own hand. So that made six.

Only Ivy was missing. 'She's over there on the duck pond,' said Holly.

'She's always been a bit of a floating voter,' said Dasher. 'But I'm sure we can get her on our side.'

Everyone agreed that by pledging their support they were now part of Timmy's Christmas party.

'Where's that Farmer Carver off to?'

'But how will we persuade Timmy's family to vote for Christmas,?' asked Noel. 'They always vote **NO** and there are so many of them!'

It was time for a **CAMPAIGN**. Gabriel and Holly brainstormed some slogans. Then Timmy's supporters put them up all over Pear Tree Farm.

TURN **NO, NO, NO!** INTO **HO, HO, HO!**

VOTE YES

CHOOSE IT OR LOSE IT!

I ♥ SANTA

'Those turkeys still don't look convinced about Christmas.'

BE MERRY AND BRIGHT: IT'S OUR RIGHT!

CHOOSE IT OR LOSE IT!

V4 XMAS

VOTE XMAS!

VOTE YES and SANTA WILL STOP HERE!

Carol said Timmy could use her milk float as the campaign bus. Everyone climbed aboard and Dasher made up a campaign anthem.

VOTE YES

VOTE

V4 XMAS

'Vote for Christmas, be a dear.
Vote for all that festive cheer.

Vote to wear your Christmas sweater.
Vote to make December better.

Vote to hear those sleigh bells ring.
Vote for cheesy songs to sing.

Do what Timmy recommends:
Vote for Christmas, my dear friends!'

'Talking of sleigh bells,
I have a cunning plan.
It involves taking a
message to Santa at the
North Pole—back soon!'

Even Ivy hopped on as the campaign bus swung past the pond. 'I've decided to back **Christmas!**' she quacked.

TURN **NO, NO, NO!**
INTO **HO, HO, HO!**

VOTE YES

The bus came to a stop outside the barn where the turkeys were having a meeting of their own.

BE MERRY AND BRIGHT: IT'S OUR RIGHT!

VOTE YES

VOTE

V4 XMAS

Loud voices could be heard coming from inside.

'I'm back. That naughty Farmer Carver is still up to no good!'

'What don't we want?'
'CHRISTMAS!'

'When don't we want it?'
'NOW!'

Dad was talking turkey. 'We need to stand firm,' he said. 'Letting Christmas happen means only one thing. And we all know what that is!'

Uncle Bernard looked wistfully through the window
at the happy faces on Timmy's campaign bus.

He had voted NO all his
life. But was it just habit?
Was it time to go . . .

BRRR! BRRR!

. . . cold turkey?

'That disguise is fooling no-one!'

VOTE

VOTE YES

'Yay, Uncle Bernard!' said Timmy. 'Welcome aboard!'

V4 XMAS

Christmas Eve arrived—and
that meant . . . **voting day!**

Everyone queued up outside
the polling station. Dad gave
Uncle Bernard a grim stare.

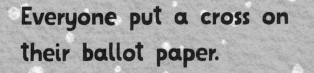

Everyone put a cross on their ballot paper.

VOTE HERE

When all the votes were in, it was time for the result.

There were **8 YES** votes and **7 NO** votes.

The animals had spoken.
It was a victory for Christmas.

'Stay calm folks—
Santa is in on this!'

VOTE HERE

YES

NO

The turkeys gasped.

'WE'RE STUFFED!'

they cried.

While Timmy, Noel, Carol, Ivy, Dasher, Holly, Gabriel . . .
and Uncle Bernard got everything ready for Christmas Day,
the other turkeys shuddered with fear.

Eventually it was time for bed . . .

. . . and in the morning, everyone woke up to the best Christmas ever on Pear Tree Farm! Santa stayed for a lovely nut roast lunch.

Then he set off for home in **Carol's** milk float.

For Zach and Tamsin with love.
Did you spot Mouse's footprints? – M.C.

For Stephen, Happy Christmas! – S.H.

OXFORD
UNIVERSITY PRESS

Great Clarendon Street, Oxford OX2 6DP
Oxford University Press is a department of the University of Oxford.
It furthers the University's objective of excellence in research, scholarship,
and education by publishing worldwide. Oxford is a registered trade mark
of Oxford University Press in the UK and in certain other countries

Text copyright © 2017 Oxford University Press
Illustrations copyright © 2017 Samara Hardy

The moral rights of the author have been asserted

Database right Oxford University Press (maker)

First published in 2017

British Library Cataloguing in Publication Data

Data available

ISBN: 978-0-19-276595-6

1 3 5 7 9 10 8 6 4 2

Printed in China

Paper used in the production of this book is a natural,
recyclable product made from wood grown in sustainable forests.
The manufacturing process conforms to the environmental
regulations of the country of origin.